ABOUT THE AUTHOR

Maggie Anderson is an Australian author who loves to write and entertain her readers. With almost twenty novels published—urban fantasy series *Dark Legacy,* four romances, and book four in the *Moon Grove Paranormal Romance Thriller* series recently released, among others. You can find read free excerpts at: www.m-anderson.com.au

BOOKS BY
MAGGIE ANDERSON

Driving Me Crazy
Love's Twist of Fate
A Night of Passion
A Night of Passion: Clean Romance Edition
Christmas, Mistletoe and You
Christmas, Mistletoe and Me

MOON GROVE PARANORMAL
ROMANCE THRILLER SERIES

Wolf Blood
Wolf Curse
Wolf Lover
Wolf Curse
Wolf Haven

URBAN FANTASY SERIES
AS M. A. ANDERSON

Reece: Prequel
Dark Legacy
Once Bitten
Soul Chaser
Evil Nature
Most Deadly

COLLECTIONS

Dark Musings

NON-FICTION

Write Your First Book

Christmas, Mistletoe and Me

MAGGIE ANDERSON

Bella Luna Books
Australia

First Edition published 2021

copyright©2021 Bella Luna Books, Australia
Brisbane, Queensland, Australia

Cover design by Maggie Anderson

Front cover photos from
shutterstock.com, pixabay.com

ISBN-13: 9780648483649

$\mathcal{P}$ROLOGUE

Kirsty Holloway was on the sidewalk, arms dripping with shopping bags and packages, waiting for the next available cab to pull into the rank. Christmas in New York was the busiest time of the year and she knew how difficult it would be to get a taxi at this time of the evening. The holiday season was her favorite celebration, so at least she could admire the twinkling white lights and other colorful festive decorations while she waited in the winter chill. The gutters were overflowing with slushy mounds of gray snow and, if she wasn't careful, when a cab pulled in she'd be sprayed with the murky freeze. Her body gave an involuntary shiver as she waited and Kirsty hoped a taxi would come by soon.

She spotted a cab heading her way and awkwardly thrust out her overladen arm to hail it, but as the vehicle pulled into the curb a guy in a dark gray overcoat whipped open the back passenger door and climbed in, mouthing 'sorry' and giving her a handsome grin through the window as the taxi merged back into the Christmas traffic chaos.

"Well, of all the nerve." Kirsty couldn't believe how inconsiderate he had been. Couldn't he see she needed the cab more than he did? And hadn't she hailed it in the first place? He'd had no shopping bags. Where was his Christmas spirit?

Kirsty could feel the flush of angry frustration spread across her icy cheeks warming them to a rosy glow. Now she'd have to wait for who knew how long for another available taxi before she could arrive home to her cozy apartment and begin the happy task of wrapping the gifts she'd bought for her family and friends. She let out a sigh and shook off the feeling; she wasn't going to allow one rude gesture to ruin her holiday cheer.

After waiting another thirty minutes for a cab, and traveling the extra half hour to her building (which should have taken ten minutes, but the traffic had been chaos), Kirsty finally stepped into her warm apartment and dropped the bundle of Christmas goodies on the floor by the front door. She'd take a hot shower to freshen up, change into her pajamas, robe, and slippers, and make a cup of hot chocolate with marshmallows before getting started on the presents.

As she sat on the sofa beside her brightly twinkling tree, Kirsty felt elated as she wrapped the gifts her family would love. She always made a point of buying something she knew they wanted and couldn't wait to see the excitement on their faces when they opened their presents on Christmas morning. She gave a contented sigh and continued her task. It was going to be a wonderful holiday… she could feel it.

The guy who'd stolen her cab popped into her head and she frowned. Why had he been so inconsiderate? It was the season of giving, after all. Her mind conjured up a picture of him. He was handsome, no doubt about that. Dark hair, blue eyes and a smile to die for, but he obviously had no manners at all. Chivalry was indeed dead. She wondered what his name was. Was he a New Yorker or in the city for the holidays? Maybe he was here visiting family. It didn't really matter because she was never going to see him again.

CHAPTER ONE

Two weeks later: A week before Christmas

Kirsty stepped into the crowded elevator heading for the fifteenth floor. She worked for Dress to Impress Magazine, a fashion exposé for the fuller-figured woman to complement their voluptuous curves, and she loved her job. Flattering women who weren't stick thin made what she did seem worthwhile. Why should slim women be the only ones to have fun with their clothes? She believed any woman should be comfortable in what they wore and enjoy the feeling of looking great no matter what their size.

Today, they would meet their new editor and chief, Sean Donovan, who was renowned for taking a once successful publication and skyrocketing sales with his innovative and creative approach. Everyone in the office was excited to see what plans he had for the magazine, and she, for one, wanted to work closely with him to learn from the best. His reputation preceded him and she couldn't wait to meet him.

When the elevator stopped at her floor only she and another passenger remained inside. As the doors slid open the man standing behind her said, "After you."

His deep, masculine voice poured over her like the warmth radiating from a burning fire and her body tingled.

"Thank you." She turned to look at him and the smile on her face stopped mid-motion. "You!"

His amazing blue eyes met hers and his smile widened. "Well, hello, I never expected to see you again."

"No, I imagine you wouldn't after hijacking my cab." She could hear the tightness in her voice and felt her spine stiffen. Of course he never expected to see her again and that's the reason why he had taken her cab in the first place.

"I'm sorry about that. I was late for an appointment. I guess I should have offered to share it with you but I was in a hurry and only thought about it after we'd driven away."

"You should've offered to share *my* cab with *me*? The cab *you* stole?"

"I am sorry. Won't you accept my apology considering we're going to be working together?"

Her eyes widened along with her mouth and she snapped it shut. So this was the famous, or infamous, Sean Donovan. Her new boss. Kirsty didn't know whether to laugh or to cry. How could this happen? "I suppose I don't have a choice, do I?"

"People always have choices, Miss Holloway." The gorgeous smile disappeared from his handsome face and he motioned for her to step out of the elevator ahead of him.

Kirsty's elated mood deflated. How could she work with a man who had no consideration for other people, especially at Christmas time? He may have offered an apology, but that was only because they'd be working together and he realized it would make the situation awkward. The incident may have been a small thing; well, actually, it wasn't such a small thing. *Who steals someone's taxi when they can see you're struggling with packages and bags?* She stepped out of the elevator without another word and made her way to her desk, knowing it was going to be a long, difficult day.

When she reached her cubicle, Allie popped up from her seat and came around the partition. "Hey, you." She greeted with a smile. When she saw the scowl on Kirsty's face she said, "What's up?"

"You remember that guy I told you about, the one who stole my cab?" Kirsty dropped her purse under her desk, peeled off her coat and scarf, and sat down.

"Yeah, why?"

"He's Sean Donovan."

Allie's mouth and eyes widened. "Our new boss? No way."

"Yes way."

"Did he recognize you?" Allie sat on the corner of Kirsty's desk and folded her arms.

"Yes. And he apologized."

"Well that's a good thing, isn't it?"

"Is it? He only did it because we have to work together. He said he never expected to see me again."

"Oh." She reached out and touched her friend's shoulder. "Don't let it get to you, hon, we have to keep things professional around here, right?"

"You're right. I know." Kirsty gave a heavy sigh. "But it isn't going to be easy."

Later that morning, everyone was called to a meeting in the boardroom. Sean had arranged a meet and greet. Kirsty's stomach squirmed as she entered the room with the eighteen foot, maple table in the center and found a seat as far away from her boss as she could. Allie came in shortly after, her eyes roaming the room, spotted Kirsty, and took the seat beside her.

"How are you doing?" she asked.

"Like you said, we have to be professional."

Allie patted her friend's knee. "Good girl. You got this."

Sean entered the room and closed the glass door. "Welcome. Thanks for being here." He remained standing. "I'd like to start by telling you a bit about myself even though I'm sure you've all Googled me." He smiled and his gaze moved to Kirsty.

She blushed and diverted her eyes.

People in the room chuckled and Kirsty ran her gaze around the smiling faces. Why hadn't she thought to do that so she wasn't blindsided when she came into work today? Damn it!

"But before we begin, I've placed some sticky labels and markers on the table. I'd appreciate it if you could write your first name on one and stick it somewhere on your front so I can address you personally during the meeting. I have looked through your personnel profiles, but right now I'm not going to immediately remember everyone's names. Thanks so much." His gaze moved briefly to Kirsty again before returning to the notes in front of him.

Allie reached over and slid a sheet of labels across the table towards herself, wrote Kirsty's name on one and passed it to her, then one for herself which she peeled and stuck on the right-hand breast pocket of her pale blue blouse. "You probably don't need one, hon. I'm sure he remembers who you are." She gave her friend a wink and a cheesy grin before turning her attention back to the eye candy at the head of the table.

Kirsty felt her cheeks flush and knew she was blushing even more than before. The meeting was going to be more difficult than she'd anticipated. "I'm pretty sure I'm not that important."

"Mm, really? Then why does he keep looking along the table at you?"

"He isn't *looking at me* as such. We didn't get off to a great start in the elevator and he's probably considering ways to fire me."

Allie waved her friend's comment off. "Don't be ridiculous. He'd be a fool to let you go. This place would fall apart if you weren't here. You know more about this magazine than anyone else I know."

"Thanks for the vote of confidence, Al, but I'm pretty certain I'm just as dispensable as the janitor."

"OMG! Let's hope they never get rid of Frank. He's a gem."

"That he is." She shrugged. "Even so, if the budget called for it…"

Allie gave Kirsty a stern stare. "You are *in*-dispensable. And don't you forget it. What would we do without you?"

Kirsty shrugged. "No one is indispensable, Al. No one."

Sean clapped his hands together twice to get everyone's attention. "Ok. All done?"

The team around the table nodded and responded with a unified yes.

"Great. Moving along. I'll give you a quick brief of where I've worked and what I've done previously and if you have any questions, please feel free to ask them at the end of the session. We'll have a Q and A then."

Sean Donovan had impressive credentials indeed and, for someone as young as he, had traveled extensively for business and pleasure. He also spoke five languages: German, French, Japanese, Spanish, and Italian. Kirsty didn't want to admire him but she couldn't help it. He was the complete package, in more ways than one.

CHAPTER TWO

Kirsty loaded her red Honda hatchback with all the gifts she'd be taking with her and also her suitcase, ready for the following morning. She was excited to be spending the holidays with her family and catching up with friends she hadn't seen in a while. Working in the city, miles away from her hometown, didn't allow for much time to make regular visits home unless it was for a special occasion. The drive would take at least five hours with the snowy conditions and she would need to be careful on the slippery roads. She loved this time of year and couldn't wait to get to her parents' house and unpack the presents under the Christmas tree, then settle in for some eggnog and Christmas movies. It was a family tradition to watch Christmas movies together during the holidays and her mom had a lovely selection of classic and modern DVDs. Kirsty's favorites were *A Mom for Christmas* and

Christmas with the Kranks, which she knew were her mom's favorites too.

As she headed back upstairs her cell played Deck the Halls in her pocket and she pulled it out to see who was calling. She frowned at the number on the screen and didn't recognize it so she pressed decline and continued up to her apartment. When she reached her front door the phone went off again… it was the same number. She stood and stared at the screen for a moment wishing it would tell her who was on the other end of the call, then pressed the answer button. "Hello?"

"Kirsty, it's Sean. I need you to come into the office tonight."

She gave a silent sigh. "I'm on vacation. Can't it wait until after the holidays?"

"The edition needs to go out overnight for tomorrow and there's a problem."

"Can't Patrick help you with it?"

"He flew out this morning heading for Australia. His family live there."

"Oh, yes, that's right." She sighed again. "I guess if it's urgent…"

"It is. Thank you, Kirsty, I appreciate it. See you soon?"

"Ok. I'll be there as soon as I can." Kirsty looked at the sparkling screensaver on her phone and gave another sigh, her holiday spirit waning just that little bit. She really didn't want to go into the office on the night before Christmas Eve, but what choice did she have?

Kirsty and Sean headed to the elevators. "Thank you for coming in on such short notice. At least now the edition will run on time." He pressed the ground floor button. "I'll make sure payroll adds the additional hours to your holiday pay."

"I'm glad I could help."

The lift doors opened and the pair stepped inside.

"Would you like to go for a coffee, my treat, for coming here so late?"

"Thanks for the offer but I've still got a few things to do before I leave in the morning."

"Oh. Sure. Ok." His gaze moved to the descending numbers above the elevator doors. "Heading home for the holidays?"

"Yes. It's really the only time I get to spend with my family, seeing as we live so far away from each other. I love going home at Christmas." Her eyes moved sideways toward him. "What about you? Are you spending the holidays with your family?"

Sean shook his head. "My parents died when I was a teenager. Car accident. And I was an only child, so…"

"I'm so sorry." She reached across and touched his arm in a gesture of compassion, but realizing it was too personal snatched her hand away.

Her boss smiled. "Thanks, but it was a long time ago. You have brothers and sisters?"

Kirsty nodded. "A sister, Kristen. She's a year older than me."

"Must be nice having a sibling."

"It is. We get along so well, always have. She's my other best friend." Kirsty smiled at the thought, then frowned. "So what are you going to do for the holidays?"

"I was raised by my aunt. We see each other on Christmas Eve. She has a busy social life and spends Christmas with a group of friends she's known for years."

"But what about Christmas day?"

"I usually work. Keeps me busy and I don't have to think about the holidays." He shrugged. "I'm used to it."

Kirsty felt bad for Sean, even though she wasn't fond of the man, she thought it was sad that he'd be spending Christmas day alone.

"Are you sure you don't have time for that coffee? It's the least I can offer considering you came into the office on your day off."

She glanced at her wristwatch. 10:00PM. "Ok. But it will have to be a quick one."

"No problem. The coffee shop is only a five minute walk away."

As she stepped into her apartment and closed the door her cell jingled. *Who could be calling at this time of night?* She snatched her phone from her purse. Allie's name appeared on the screen. "Hey, what's up?"

"Nothing. I just wanted to wish you a very merry Christmas and to say be safe on the road. You're my best friend and I love you."

"Aw, that's sweet. You know I love you, too."

"Yeah, I do. So are you all packed and ready?"

"Not quite. I still have a few things to do before I'm totally ready to leave."

"How come? You're usually so well organized by now."

"Sean called. I had to go into the office. There was a malfunction in the system and he couldn't upload the magazine edition that had to be run overnight."

"Couldn't Patrick have helped with that?"

"He's on a flight to Australia, so no."

"Oh? And did you guys fix the problem?"

"Yeah. The edition is running as we speak. Thank goodness. If it hadn't I might not have been going home for the holidays."

"So what's he like one on one?"

"You know, he's not as bad as I first thought. We actually talked about some personal stuff, which was kind of nice."

"Really? What kind of personal stuff?" There was definitely a suspicious overtone to her friend's voice. And Kirsty knew what that meant.

"Nothing like what you're thinking. He told me his parents passed away when he was a teenager and that he was raised by his aunt. They see each other on Christmas Eve but he works on Christmas day. How sad is that?"

"So he spends the holidays alone?"

"Yes."

"Wow. I would've thought he'd have women lining up to spend Christmas with him."

"Allie."

"What? He's a great looking guy. Surely he has women friends."

"I have no idea. We didn't discuss our love lives."

"Well maybe you should have. At least you'd know if he was single or not."

"And why would I care? He's my boss."

"Come on, Kirsty, I'm your best friend. I know you. You already like him, don't you?"

"Not like that. He's a nice man. Not at all what I thought he was like. He volunteers at a homeless shelter, that's what he meant by work."

"On Christmas day?"

"Yes. So I guess he's not totally alone. Isn't that admirable?"

"Yeah. How did you find that out?"

"We went for coffee after we finished at the office."

"You did? Did *he* ask you?"

"He did. He said it was the least he could do after having me come in on my vacation time, which he intends to pay me for."

"So I was right."

Kirsty frowned. "What are you talking about?"

"That day in the boardroom when he kept glancing at you. He likes you, Kirsty."

"Don't be ridiculous."

"I'm serious. Why else would he ask you for coffee?"

"To say thank you for helping him out in a tight spot."

"Believe what you like. I know these things."

Kirsty chuckled. "Sure. Ok. I need to go and finish organizing for the morning. I've got a bit to catch up on before I go to bed. Have a wonderful Christmas and I'll see you in two weeks. Hope you like your present. Love you."

"Hope you like yours, too. Love you back."

They always exchanged gifts early – because Kirsty traveled home for the holidays – but didn't open them until midday on Christmas day, so they opened them together even though they were in different parts of the country. It had become their Christmas friendship tradition.

CHAPTER THREE

Kirsty pulled into the drive of her parents' two story, gray and white, cottage style house a little after midday and gave a relieved sigh. It was good to be off the roads and home again. She loved spending the holidays with her family, and catching up with friends she grew up with who still lived in the town. The time away from the city refreshed her and always seemed to give her a new perspective on the things that really mattered. Not that she didn't already know. Loved ones were the most important people in her life.

Kirsty opened the car door and stepped out, breathing in the crisp winter air. A plume of white escaping her lips as she exhaled.

The front door opened and her mom rushed down the front porch steps to greet her, arms wide. "Hi, honey, it's good to see you. Merry Christmas." She wrapped her daughter in her loving embrace and hugged her tight.

"It's good to be home, Mom. Merry Christmas to you, too." Her gaze moved to the open front door. "Where's dad? And Kristen?"

"Dad's in the garage gathering more wood for the fire and your sister's in the kitchen baking treats for tomorrow."

"Gingerbread and sugar cookies?"

"Yes."

At that moment, her sister came out onto the porch, giving Kirsty a big smile and wave. "Hey, sis, it's good to have you home."

"It's good to be here."

Kirsty and her mom moved around to the rear of her hatchback and tugged the luggage and big bag of gifts from the trunk.

"Let's get you inside out of the cold and I'll make us all some hot chocolate."

"With marshmallows?" Kirsty asked, eyebrows raised.

Her mother nodded. "With marshmallows. Is there any other way to drink it?"

As they entered the house, Kirsty gave her sister a tight hug. She'd missed her. Kristen's husband, Brady, was a police officer, so he was most likely working. "Is Brady here?"

Kristen shook her head. "He's on duty today."

"But he'll be here for Christmas, right?"

Her sister smiled. "Yes, he has Christmas day off, thank goodness."

Kirsty patted her sister's bulging baby belly. "Not long now. I can't wait to meet my little niece or nephew." Her sister knew the gender of the baby but didn't want to reveal it until their bundle of joy arrived. She wanted it to be a surprise for the family. Like in the old days.

"Me neither. I've loved being pregnant but can't wait until the baby's here. These days I feel like a beached whale." She chuckled.

The pair headed into the kitchen.

Kirsty made her sister sit down while she took the last batch of cookies out of the oven. They smelled divine and she breathed in the sugary goodness. "Mm. You are the best baker I know." Her shoulders rose and she grimaced. "But don't tell mom I said that."

Kristen laughed. "I won't."

At that moment, her father appeared in the doorway. "Hey, sweet pea, how are ya?"

Kirsty rushed across the kitchen, wrapped her arms around her dad and gave him a huge hug. "Hi, Daddy. I'm great. What about you?"

"Oh, can't complain." He smiled. "Besides, your mother keeps me on my toes."

"Glad to hear it."

"So, who's up for some hot chocolate with marshmallows?" Her mother said, entering the kitchen from the laundry.

Everyone said 'me.'

"Then it's unanimous." Christine smiled. "Tom, would you grab some mugs, oh, and the marshmallows from the pantry please?"

"Sure, honey."

Everyone sat in the living room in front of the roaring fire crackling away in the fireplace and drank their hot chocolate. These were the moments that made Christmas special. Time together as a family. They chatted and laughed and played board games together for most of the afternoon until Christine checked her watch and realized they hadn't eaten lunch. "Oh dear, look at the time, I've got to go make us something to eat."

Tom gently grabbed his wife's arm. "It's all taken care of."

"What? What do you mean?" She gave him and the girls a confused stare.

"Kirsty and Kristen already prepared something for lunch. It's in the refrigerator." Tom stood. "Shall we?"

The group wandered into the kitchen and Kirsty set the table, making sure her sister and mother sat and relaxed.

Christine jumped to her feet. "Let me help you with that."

Kirsty shook her head. "You do too much at Christmastime, Mom. Sit, relax, I've got this."

Tom helped his daughter with the bowls of food and then sat down with his family to eat. It felt good being a family unit once again. Not that he didn't like his son-in-law, he did, but it was nice having his girls all to himself for just a little while.

After lunch, the group headed back to the living room to watch some movies. Brady had called earlier to say he'd be home in time for dinner. His captain had given him and a couple of other officers the rest of the day off so they could spend it with their families. It was Christmas Eve, after all.

"Which movie will we watch first?" Kirsty asked, running her gaze over the selection of DVDs sitting on the shelves of the entertainment cabinet beside the television.

"Why don't you pick?" Christine offered, settling back on the sofa, Tom wrapping his arm around her shoulder.

"Ok." Kirsty selected a movie, popped it into the DVD player, then took a seat in one of the armchairs in front of the window, Kristen in the one beside her.

When the movie began, her mom gave a pleased gasp. White Christmas was another of her favorites. Christine glanced over at her daughter and smiled. "Thank you, honey."

Kirsty settled back in her chair, pulling her socked feet up onto the seat and gave her mom a pleased grin. "It's a beautiful Christmas classic. How could we not watch it?"

Chapter Four

Spending time with her family had been just what she'd needed to get back to work after the holidays. Christmas with the people she loved always gave her a boost and she knew that when she walked into the office the next morning she would be ready and rearing to go on her new project. Sean popped into her head as she made toast and coffee in her tiny kitchen. What would the New Year hold in respect to their working relationship? Kirsty now knew he wasn't that self-absorbed guy she'd pictured in her mind the evening he had whipped into her hailed cab and drove away. She'd even picked up a small gift for him at the Christmas market she and her family had gone to after their movie watching afternoon, and hoped he liked it. She imagined he had everything he wanted in life and thought, that perhaps, it was cheesy, but decided to give it to him anyway. Did guys like snow globes?

The doorbell gave her a start, and she dropped her piece of buttered toast onto the plate, stood up and crossed the living room. Peering through the peephole, a broad grin spread across her face and she opened the door. "Hey you," she said, wrapping her arms around her friend. "It's so good to see you."

Allie stepped into the small, cozy apartment, shrugging out of her blue wool, knee-length jacket, burgundy knit cap and scarf. "It's good to see you too. How's your family?"

"They're great. My sister is due to have her baby soon, which is exciting. I'll be an aunt."

"That's awesome." Allie crossed the room to the dining table and sat down.

Kirsty went back to her chair and sat opposite her friend. "Looking forward to getting back into our new project?"

"Yeah, I think it'll be a lot of fun... and hard work. But totally worth it."

Kirsty smiled. "Me too. Want some coffee?"

"Sure." Allie raised her hand in a stop motion. "You finish your breakfast. I'll get it." She poured herself a mug of freshly brewed coffee and rejoined her friend at the table. "Heard from Sean?"

Kirsty frowned. "No. Why would I?"

"Oh, just wondering." Allie gave Kirsty a sheepish grin.

"I told you it's not like that. He's my boss. You know that old saying about mixing business with pleasure, don't you?"

Allie shrugged. "Eh. Whoever said that didn't have a clue." She sipped her coffee. "But you do like him. Don't you?"

"He's a nice man. Yes, I like him but not in the way you mean." Kirsty finished her toast and swallowed the last mouthful of coffee in her mug, then stood up and took her dishes into the kitchen. "Besides, who knows, he may have a girlfriend."

Allie's eyebrows rose. "One who didn't spend the holidays with him? I don't think so."

Kirsty sat down again. "Well it doesn't matter anyway because I'm going to take that advice about not mixing business with pleasure. It's a whole lot easier that way."

"Suit yourself, but I think you're missing out on something that could be nice for you… and him, especially if he doesn't have a girlfriend. You're a great catch."

"What if he's gay?"

"Phftt, not likely." Allie chuckled.

"You never know. Masculine guys can be gay. Lots are."

"I doubt it. The way he was looking at you that day in the meeting…"

"Means absolutely nothing." Kirsty stood up. "Are we going shopping or not?"

Allie stood her mug in the kitchen sink. "Of course. Who would pass up a day of shopping?"

Macy's in Brooklyn Heights was quite busy with shoppers clambering for the marked down sale items throughout the store. That had been the reason Kirsty and Allie were there. Kirsty wanted to pick up a few new tops and skirts for work and a couple of casual outfits for the weekends. She also needed at least one party dress because she knew the magazine would throw a huge New Year's Eve party and, this year, she was going to attend. *Is it because Sean will be there?* she wondered, and shrugged the thought off when a gorgeous, silver sequined cocktail dress displayed on a mannequin caught her eye. "Oh, my goodness!" she exclaimed, rushing up to it, breathless. "Isn't it just…?"

Allie's gaze moved to the model standing on a cube in the center of the aisle. "That would look awesome on you." She glanced around for a saleswoman and raised her hand when she spotted one. "Excuse me." The woman ignored her. "Uh, excuse me."

The woman looked up and gave her a perfunctory smile. "Yes, can I help you?" she said, walking up to the pair.

"Can my friend try this on?"

The saleswoman's gaze moved from Allie to Kirsty. "It may be too small. It's a size two. Let me see if I have any out back." She ran her eyes up Kirsty's frame. "You'd be a size three, wouldn't you?"

"Um, yes. Thanks." Her eyes met her friend's and they both gave a quiet chuckle.

"Talk about unenthusiastic customer service."

"Can't really blame her. With Christmas just gone and the New Year sales about to start she's probably had enough of holiday shoppers for now." Kirsty looked up at the dress again and gave a soft sigh. It was perfect.

"Let's try some perfume while we wait," Allie offered.

"Good idea."

They walked over to the fragrances counter and began spraying some of the expensive brands onto cards and sniffing.

The woman returned with a dress on a hanger, but it wasn't the same one. It was champagne and sequined, but didn't have the shape or style to the one on the mannequin. "I'm sorry but we don't have any more of those in stock. There is this one though."

Kirsty's happy expression fell. "Oh. Um, no. Sorry. I don't like that one."

Allie's eyes moved back to the dress on the model. "I think that one would fit you." She turned to the saleswoman. "Would you mind getting that one down for my friend so she can try it on?"

The woman let out a soft sigh and pasted the pleasant smile back on her face. "Of course. Just give me a moment to return this one and I'll be right back."

Kirsty glanced sideways at her friend. "If looks could kill."

"Yeah." She shrugged. "Oh well, that's what she's paid to do so…"

The saleswoman went straight to the mannequin on her return, unpinned the dress, unzipped it and removed it. "Follow me, please."

Kirsty followed the woman over to the fitting rooms, Allie close behind her.

Once the dress was hung on a hook inside the cubicle, the woman left, telling them she'd return momentarily to see how the fitting went.

Kirsty tried on the dress, opened the cubicle curtain and asked her friend how it looked.

"Wow! Just wow." Allie's eyes grew wide. "You look amazing. And it fits perfectly. Pity the saleswoman hadn't just gotten it down in the first place. Would've saved a whole lotta time."

Kirsty's gaze moved past Allie and her friend knew the woman was standing behind her. Her cheeks flushed pink and she swallowed hard.

"Well, it looks like a perfect fit," the woman said. "How would you like to pay for the dress? Cash or card?"

Kirsty checked the price tag. Even though it was half price it was still out of her budget. If she wanted to buy it she'd have to put it on her card. One she only just finished paying off. She gave a heavy sigh. "Uh, would you give me a minute and I'll be right out."

"Of course." The saleswoman left the pair and headed back to her counter.

Allie frowned. "What's the matter?"

"I can't afford it." She held out the price tag for her friend to see.

"Yikes!"

"Yes." Kirsty glanced at her reflection in the mirror and bit her bottom lip. It was a gorgeous dress, and she looked amazing in it. *What would Sean think?* The thought popped into her head before she could stop it. "Unzip me, please."

"Oh, hon, I'm so sorry." She gave her friend a pained look.

"Maybe the other dress she showed us is cheaper."

"Yeah, cheaper and uglier."

Kirsty sighed again. "Yeah, I know." She stepped out of the dress, held it up in front of her and looked longingly at it. "But this one is way out of my price range."

"You could credit it."

"I know I could but I'd prefer not to."

"Ok, hon. Get dressed and I'll shout us lunch."

"Thanks." Kirsty gave her a thin smile and closed the curtain.

Sitting in the cozy warmth of the corner café, Kirsty pined over the dress she couldn't afford. She realized she wanted to make an impression on Sean, and that she did like him. The impulse to go back to Macy's and purchase the dress was pulsing through her like adrenalin. Should she?

Allie reached across the table and rested her hand on her friend's arm. "Still thinking about the dress, huh?"

Kirsty shifted on her chair. "No, well, yes… it was so lovely."

"It was. And it looked great on you."

"Thanks." She sighed. "But… like I said, I really can't afford to put it on credit."

"I know." Allie gave her friend another pained look. "Do you have any savings you could use instead?"

"Not at the moment. Christmas wiped me out."

"Oh."

"Let's not think about it anymore, ok?" She shrugged off her glum feeling. "We got everything else we wanted so…"

"We did. And at bargain prices." Allie smiled.

"Exactly. A good day's shopping, all in all." She still couldn't get that dress out of her head, though.

CHAPTER FIVE

The next morning, Kirsty dressed in one of her new outfits, applied just the right amount of makeup to look fresh and glowing, and headed to the office. She wanted to make a good impression on her boss... in more ways than one, and she wanted to give him the gift she'd picked out for him.

Smiling to herself as she approached his office, she stopped short when she could hear a conversation taking place inside. The door stood ajar. When she turned to leave, she overheard something that made her blood turn to ice water.

"Things on this assignment haven't gone according to plan, I'm afraid," Sean said.

Kirsty sidled up to the open doorway, leaning in to hear what was being said. She knew she shouldn't but couldn't help herself.

"I know, I know. And it should've made some progress by now but it hasn't. We're going to have to consider some cutbacks. But we'll wait until after the New Year party; maybe leave it until the first week of January to announce it. Ok, leave it with me."

Kirsty gave a quiet gasp. Sean was thinking about cutting staff. How could he even consider it? Everyone in the office gave one hundred and fifty percent each and every day. Her eyes glistened as she listened to the one-sided conversation taking place over the phone. It seemed to her he *was* the man she thought he was to begin with. She turned on her heel and headed back to her desk, tugged open the drawer and set the snow globe gift inside and closed the drawer with a quiet bang.

Allie came over to her. "What's wrong? You look like you just lost your best friend, which you haven't because I'm still here."

Kirsty shook her head. "It's nothing. I'd rather not talk about it right now, if that's ok?"

"Sure. But if you change your mind…"

"Yes, if I do I'll come talk to you."

Kirsty was in a funk for the rest of the day and was glad when five o'clock finally came around so she could leave. She'd avoided Sean all day, even when he'd left a message asking her to come see him. He'd been busy and hadn't had time to come over to her desk, which she was grateful for. She knew she couldn't avoid talking to him forever, but while she could she would.

When she arrived home, a beautiful bunch of red roses wrapped in iridescent pearl white paper were sitting outside her door. She frowned as she picked up the huge bouquet, tugged the tiny white envelope from the long stems, and opened the card.

Just a small token of appreciation for assisting me in a crisis situation during your time off. Sean.

He had written the card himself and had lovely handwriting, she noticed.

Pushing the key into the lock, her hands full, Kirsty shouldered the door back and stepped into her apartment. How could she accept such an extravagant gift when people were about to lose their jobs?

Crossing the living room to the kitchen, she tugged open a cupboard door, took out the crystal vase her mother had given her for her birthday a couple of years ago, and half-filled it with water. She opened the wrapping, cut the band holding the bunch of roses together, and arranged them in the vase, giving a heavy sigh as she sat it on the dining room table. Under any other circumstances, she'd believe he was making his feelings known, but as it stood now, she couldn't even consider going out with him. Not after what she had heard today.

Her cell jingled the Christmas carol she'd set for the holidays and she tugged it from her purse. Unknown caller. She frowned at the screen for a moment, contemplating whether to answer it or not, then decided she should. "Hello?"

"Hi, Kirsty, it's Sean. I wanted to check and see if you got my gift."

"Uh, yes, thank you. The flowers are lovely. You really didn't have to…"

"I know. I just wanted to say thank you again for your assistance. It was, and is still appreciated."

"I'm happy I could help."

"Me too." He waited a beat, then said, "I'd like to invite you to dinner. Would you be open to that? I usually prefer to speak face to face when it comes to inviting someone out, but we didn't get a chance to catch up at work today so I thought I'd give you a call."

Silence. What could she say? No? He was her boss. If she didn't play it cool she might be one of the cut backs.

"Kirsty, are you there?"

"Yes, I'm here."

"What do you think? Dinner?"

"Sure. I'd love to. When did you have in mind?"

"Tomorrow night, after work. We could make it an early one."

"Sounds good," she said.

"I'll book a table and let you know tomorrow where we're going."

"Do I need to dress up?"

"What you wear to the office will be fine. Neat casual."

"Ok, great. See you in the morning."

"Yes, see you then."

Kirsty rang off and let out a huge sigh. Before she knew what Sean had planned she would have been overjoyed that he'd asked her out. Why did things always have to be so complicated when it came to relationships? How could she pretend she hadn't heard what he'd said over the phone? She didn't have a choice. She wasn't meant to overhear his conversation about firing people, was she? So she had to keep it to herself.

She'd stopped in at the Lychee Nut café on the way home, but realized she had lost her appetite. Popping the plastic bag containing the food into the refrigerator, she headed for her bedroom to get ready for bed before snuggling up on the sofa to watch a movie, if she could get her mind off Sean and what he'd said.

CHAPTER SIX

Sean wasn't in the office when Kirsty arrived, which was unlike him. Perhaps he had a face to face meeting with whoever he'd been speaking to on the phone the day before. Who knew? She crossed the workspace to her desk and plonked herself down on her chair. She was doing this. She was actually going to dinner with the man she had wanted to get to know, but now wasn't at all sure about. Had she misunderstood what she'd heard? Sean seemed keen to get the magazine back to its former glory, which he had done with other waning companies, so why would he want to let people go?

Allie crossed the corridor to greet her friend. "Morning, hon."

Kirsty swung around on her swivel chair. "Hi, how's things?"

"Things are great. What about you?"

She sighed. "Yeah, things are good."

Allie frowned and folded her arms. "Doesn't sound like it to me. Are you ok?"

"I – I… Sean asked me to dinner."

Her friend's face lit up, her eyes wide, her mouth gaping. "He did? Well that's awesome. Right?"

"It would have been if…"

Allie grabbed her chair and wheeled it across the aisle. "Ok, what's up?"

"I can't tell you."

"Why not?"

"Because it's… it's none of my business."

Her friend's frown deepened. "I don't understand."

"I overheard something I wasn't meant to and it changed my opinion of Sean."

Allie rubbed her friend's arm. "It can't be that bad. Can it?"

Kirsty nodded. "Yes, it can."

"Well, now you've got me intrigued. Come on, spill."

"I can't. Believe me, it's better you don't know."

"That bad, huh?"

"That bad."

"Oh, dear. What are you going to do?"

Kirsty shrugged. "Go to dinner. What else?"

"But…"

At that moment, Sean's face appeared above the partition. "Morning, ladies." He smiled at them both. "Kirsty, can I have a word in my office please?"

Allie wheeled her chair back to her desk and watched Kirsty follow Sean across the room.

Once inside his office, with the door closed, he offered her a seat before rounding his desk and sitting down.

Kirsty clasped her hands on her lap and waited for him to speak.

"I've arranged a table at The Restaurant on ninth. Does that suit you?"

She leaned forward on her chair. "I'm not going to be able to make it tonight. I'm sorry, but something's come up."

Sean's right eyebrow arched. "Oh, I hope it's nothing serious."

She shook her head. "No, but it's something I can't get out of. Maybe we can make it another time?"

"Of course. I'll look forward to it." His smile was dazzling and Kirsty felt butterflies in the pit of her stomach. Was she doing the right thing?

"Thank you for understanding." She stood up.

"No." He waved her comment off. "I appreciate you telling me. Let me know when you're free and I'll book

47

someplace nicer." His gaze followed her across the room and out the door.

Allie rolled herself across the aisle the minute Kirsty returned to her desk. "So how'd it go? What happened?"

"I canceled our dinner date."

Her friend's eyebrows rose. "You did?"

"I told him I had something come up that I couldn't get out of."

"You know he's going to ask you again, don't you?"

Kirsty sighed and shrugged. "What else can I do?"

"You can't keep putting him off forever."

"I know. But I can for now."

Later that afternoon, as Kirsty waited on the sidewalk for a cab, Sean drove up the steep incline from the building's parking garage, stopped, and rolled down the passenger side window on his red Chevrolet Camaro. "Hey, Kirsty, need a ride?"

Kirsty pretended not to hear him at first, but after his second call to her she turned around and walked over to the car. "Hi. What did you say?"

"Do you need a ride home? I'd be happy to drive you." There was that gorgeous smile again that made her heart flutter.

"Oh, no, that's ok. I wouldn't want to put you out."

"It's no imposition at all. Climb in."

Kirsty groaned inwardly, opened the door and got into the car.

"Just give me your address and I'll get you there in no time. Better than waiting for a cab or a bus."

She gave him a thin smile. "Thanks. I appreciate it." She told him her address and he keyed it into the satnav.

"Buckle up."

Kirsty tugged the seatbelt over her shoulder, clipped it in, and sat back wishing she'd hailed a cab before Sean had left. The drive home would be uncomfortable and awkward.

As they drove toward Kirsty's address, Sean glanced at her sideways. He liked her and hoped she liked him too. He thought, perhaps, she did, but one could never be sure when it came to affairs of the heart, and he wasn't one to assume anything. He'd been engaged once to the woman he'd hoped to spend the rest of his life with, but she'd cheated on him and turned his world upside down. Many of his friends had tried to match him up with single ladies, but he'd needed time to make sense of what had happened and to move on before even contemplating starting a new relationship with anyone. Kirsty seemed like a lovely young woman and someone he'd really like to get to know, but he wasn't about to make the same mistake again. He'd take it slow and steady.

"Not far now," he said, giving her a smile.

"I really appreciate you doing this. I hope it isn't too far out of your way."

"Not at all," he lied. It was a white lie so she wouldn't feel bad about the fact he had to head back in the opposite direction. After a few more minutes, he pulled his sports car into the curb outside a triple-story apartment building. "Here we are, safe and sound."

Kirsty released her seatbelt, picked up her purse, and opened the door. "Thank you."

His beautiful blue eyes met hers. "It was my pleasure."

She closed the door and gave him a wave as he pulled out into the street. Was he the bad guy she thought him to be? Or was she mistaken? She needed to find out one way or the other.

CHAPTER SEVEN

Sleep was impossible. Kirsty tossed and turned, lay on her back and stared up at the ceiling, her thoughts filled with Sean Donovan. Maybe she should just come right out and ask him if he plans to let people go in the New Year. She cringed at the thought because she hadn't been meant to hear that conversation. She had been eavesdropping and, that in itself, could get her fired. She let out a heavy sigh and rolled over, knowing she wouldn't sleep. She couldn't help the way she felt about him, so what was she to do?

When Kirsty finally drifted into a restless sleep, Sean's face appeared and woke her with a start. Glancing at the digital bedside clock, she gave another heavy sigh. 4:00AM. If she didn't get a couple hours sleep she'd look like a zombie in the morning. She turned over onto her left side, closed her eyes and willed herself to sleep… without dreams, she hoped.

The continuous annoying beep of the alarm pulled Kirsty from the short sleep she managed to get. Dragging herself out of bed, she headed for the shower to help wake her up. As she stepped into the warm spray, she wondered if she should ask him. But how to approach the topic without him realizing she'd heard what he'd said over the phone?

Skipping breakfast, as she didn't feel hungry at all, Kirsty marched out the front door of her apartment and headed for the taxi rank down the street. She'd consider her options about speaking to Sean and see what she could come up with. The only way to know the truth would be to ask him.

As she stepped out of the elevator, Allie rushed over to her, her face ashen. "Kirsty, have you heard?"

Kirsty gave her friend a confused look. "Heard about what?"

"About Sean."

She frowned. "No. What about him?"

"He was involved in a car accident and is in the hospital."

"What?!"

"I know."

"Is – is he ok?"

"No one knows. That's all we've heard so far."

"When did it happen?"

"Yesterday evening."

"Oh no!" Kirsty's heart raced and her throat tightened. Had he had the accident because he'd offered to drive her home? "Which hospital is he in?"

"The one on York Avenue."

Kirsty jabbed the elevator call button.

Allie frowned at her. "What are you going to do?"

"I'm going there to find out how he is."

"They won't tell you anything because you're not family."

Kirsty swung around. Her friend was right. "Then how are we supposed to know how he's doing?"

Allie shrugged. "I don't know. Maybe someone will fill us in when they send in a replacement."

A replacement?

"They will, won't they? Especially if he needs recuperation time." Kirsty frowned then her face brightened. "I'll tell the nursing staff I'm his fiancée."

"Kirsty."

"It's the only way to find out how he is and if he'll be coming back."

"I don't know if that's a good idea."

Kirsty gripped her friend's arms. "It's the only way."

"I hope you're right about that."

Kirsty walked up to the nurse's station and stood at the counter watching a nurse on a call. Once the call ended the young woman glanced up at her with a smile. "Are you here to see a patient?"

Mustering up the courage she needed to do this, Kirsty said, "Yes. Sean Donovan."

The nurse typed the name into the computer then returned her gaze to Kirsty. "Are you family?"

"I – I… I'm his fiancée."

The nurse frowned and looked at the information on the screen. "We have his next of kin as his aunt."

"Oh, well, yes, she is his blood relative. She would be considered his next of kin. Once we're married that will change."

"Ok, well, he's resting at the moment. The doctor has been to see him this morning. He has a mild concussion and broken leg, a few scrapes and bruises, but other than that he's reasonably ok. We kept him in overnight for observation, just to be sure."

"I appreciate the wonderful care he's receiving here. Can I see him?"

"Of course. Room 313." She pointed along the corridor. "Second last on the left."

"Thank you so much." Kirsty smiled then turned and headed down the bright passage.

When she reached the door, she stopped, inhaled a deep breath and let it out slowly. She had lied her way into his room. Would his aunt be in there with him? Kirsty pushed the door open and stepped inside. *Wow! This is what private health cover can afford.* She closed the door and walked over to the bed. Sean looked so fragile right now. A tear slipped down her left cheek and she brushed it away.

Pulling up the chair next to the bed, she sat and watched him as he slept. She didn't have the heart to wake him after everything he'd been through.

The room was lovely. Large window with a view. Mint colored walls. Comfortable bed, for a hospital bed, and all the amenities one could ask for.

Sean stirred and opened his eyes, his face covered with an oxygen mask. His gaze moved to her. "Kirsty?"

She stood up and came over to the bed. "Hi."

"Hi." He frowned. "What…"

"Am I doing here?" She reached out and took his hand in hers. "I had to know you were ok."

"But, how…?" He tugged the clear rubber mask under his chin.

"That's an interesting story, actually." She chuckled nervously.

"Don't get me wrong, it's great to see you, but they only allow family to visit in these kinds of circumstances."

"Yes, I'm aware."

"So?"

"I – I lied. I told the nurse I was your fiancée." Her cheeks flushed pink.

An amused smile spread across his injured, handsome face. "Clever."

Her eyes widened. "You're not mad at me?"

"Why would I be mad at someone who used ingenuity to get the job done?" His smile grew wider.

"Phew! I'm so relieved." She realized she was still holding his hand and eased hers out of his.

"Hey, I'm injured. I need comfort." He gave her a wink.

She smiled. "You'll live, apparently."

"Well that's good news."

"You'll need time to recuperate so I guess the hierarchy will send someone else in while you're on leave." Her face dropped.

"Not if I can help it. It's a broken leg. I can still work."

"You really do need to get well."

"I'm fine. Lucky, but fine."

"Well that's something you'll need to discuss with the big boss, I guess."

"And I will. I never shirk my responsibilities."

"I understand that, but this is different, Sean. You were involved in a car accident. One that was probably my fault."

Sean reached out and gripped her hand. "No, it wasn't. The road was icy, another car hit me. It was an accident. Please don't blame yourself. You had nothing to do with it."

He'd been traveling home after dropping her off. Of course she had something to do with it. She nodded without a word, and swallowed the guilt aching in her throat.

CHAPTER EIGHT

Within a week, Sean was back in the office on crutches. He was a man of his word, Kirsty realized, one who, as he'd said, didn't shirk his responsibilities. She was glad he was ok. He had asked her to assist him for the next few weeks, so she would be his PA of sorts while he mended and worked, and she had jumped at the opportunity to spend time with him one on one. The nagging feeling that had bothered her since she'd heard his phone conversation was still sitting in the back of her mind, but it would have to wait.

She enjoyed working with him. They had a lot in common, she discovered, and always seemed to be laughing together. She liked the way he made her feel and hope the feeling was mutual.

At lunch, that afternoon, Allie and Kirsty sat together in the office cafeteria. They hadn't had a chance to catch up over the past week, so it was as good a time as any.

"How's it going?" Allie asked.

"Good." Kirsty forked the salad around her plate but didn't take a bite.

Her friend gave her a curious frown. "Ok. So if it's good why do you look like you lost your best friend? Again, I'm still here."

"It's, well, I still know what I know about him."

"So talk to him. Ask him or whatever needs to be done to resolve the issue. You like him, anyone can see he likes you, so do something about it, hon."

"I know you're right, and I should, but I wanted to wait until he's completely well again. It would only be added stress for him."

"He doesn't seem too stressed to me."

"That's because he hides it well."

"Well, you'd know more than I would, at this point. You're the one spending time with him."

"I *will* do something about it, just not right now."

"And in the meantime you're going to pine over it."

"I won't."

Allie wrapped her fingers around her friend's hand. "You will. I know you."

59

That night, back in her apartment, Kirsty sat at the dining table picking at the take out she'd ordered before leaving the office, and wondered what she could say to Sean about what she'd heard. Allie was right. She needed to resolve the issue once and for all, otherwise it would ruin any chance of her and Sean having a relationship, which seemed to be the direction their friendship was heading.

It was time to fess up and to ask him if he was putting people off. Her stomach did an anxious flip flop under the waistband of her black linen pants and she pushed the container of food away from her. Maybe she should just put it to bed and forget she ever heard that conversation. Should she? Could she? No, her conscience wouldn't let her.

Kirsty took the remaining food out to the kitchen and spooned it into plastic containers, placing them in the refrigerator. She'd suddenly lost her appetite.

As she headed for the bedroom, her cell jingled. She hadn't yet removed the Christmas carol on it and should, now that it was almost the New Year. The party was tomorrow evening and she realized she still didn't have anything new to wear. She would just have to rehash something she'd worn to a previous bash and jazz it up with some accessories.

Checking the screen, she noticed it was her mom. "Hey, Mom, how's things?"

"Hi, honey. I just wanted to let you know your sister had the baby a few minutes ago. It's a beautiful baby boy."

"Oh, Mom, that's wonderful. So they're going with Gabriel Gene?"

"I think so. I didn't ask. Mom and bub are doing great." She waited a moment, then said, "Can you get away to come visit?"

"Oh, Mom, I wish I could but I'm swamped right now."

"That's ok, honey, I understand. We'll send photos soon. I'd better go. Love you."

"I'd love to see some pics. Tell Kristen I'm so happy for her and Brady and can't wait to meet my little nephew when I can get away. Thanks for letting me know. Love you too."

Kirsty couldn't wipe the smile of joy off her face. A new member of their family was such a wonderful, joyful thing. She was an aunt. She made a mental note to send flowers tomorrow, and then headed to bed.

CHAPTER NINE

NEW YEAR'S EVE

Kirsty stepped into the beautiful ballroom decked out in gold and silver balloons, tinsel, streamers, with glitter sprinkled on the table tops, floors and any other surface within the expansive room. Instrumentals played in the background, and people were milling around in small groups drinking champagne and talking. Laughter rang out throughout the hall. Everyone was having a wonderful time.

She realized that expensive sequined dress she had so wanted to buy would have been perfect for tonight, but decided to put it out of her mind. She had chosen to wear a little black dress, cut just above the knee, with a spaghetti strap top and had accessorized with gold jewelry, necklace with a dangling heart, earrings to match, and a couple of bracelets. Her purse was gold as well but she had chosen black stilettos to finish the look. She had piled her hair up in a soft chignon and pushed a gold and cubic zirconia butterfly clip into her brunette curls.

Allie came rushing across the floor to her, two champagne flutes in hand. "Hey, hon, glad you're here." She reached around carefully and gave her friend a hug, then passed her a drink. "To a fun night."

They clinked glasses and sipped the bubbly.

Kirsty's gaze roamed the people in the room. Allie noticed.

"He hasn't arrived yet. Anyway, why didn't you two come together?"

"It was my idea. We're keeping it on the down low. You're the only one in the office that knows."

Allie chuckled. "Uh, I hate to tell you this, but everyone knows."

"And here I thought I was doing such a good job of hiding it." Kirsty smiled.

"News travels fast around the office. You should know that by now."

Patrick crossed the glistening parquet wooden floor to the pair. "Hey, it's a great night, don't you think?"

"Yeah, it is. I'm starved though. I wonder when they're serving food." Allie took another sip of her champagne.

Patrick's gaze moved to the empty white covered tables with beautiful sprays of sunflowers, lilies and ferns. "Yeah, me too. If we don't get food soon I'm willing to have a bite of a sunflower." He chuckled.

"Let's hope it won't come to that," Kirsty said, smiling.

"Well I'm off to mingle. Catch you later." Patrick turned on his heel.

"Yeah, see you." Both women said together.

"I'm so glad you sorted out that little problem you had." Allie finished her bubbly.

Kirsty gave her a sheepish glance.

"Oh no. Don't tell me you didn't."

"Things have been going so well. Why spoil it?"

"Because you need to clear the air if this relationship is going to work, hon. I don't have to tell you that."

"I know, I know."

All of a sudden, everyone in the room started clapping. Sean had arrived, fashionably late.

He raised his hands to quiet the crowd and was handed a microphone. "Thank you, everyone. It's great to be here tonight to celebrate the coming New Year with you all. I look forward to getting around to each of you throughout the evening. In the meantime, please enjoy the festivities." He handed the mic back to the woman standing behind him, glanced around the ballroom for Kirsty and came across to her and Allie. "Hi." His appraising gaze roamed her slim frame. "You look lovely."

"Thank you. You do too. I mean handsome."

"Thanks."

Allie stood for a moment, then said. "I'm going to go grab some more champagne."

Once her friend had left, Kirsty turned to Sean. "Can we talk somewhere quiet?"

He frowned into her eyes. "Sure. Follow me."

The pair stepped through a double wooden door into a private lounge area.

"Is something wrong?" Sean asked.

"I need to tell you something."

"Oh. What is it?"

"Can we sit?"

"Of course." He motioned for her to take a seat on the brown leather buttoned sofa and joined her. "What's the matter? You look like you've lost your best friend."

She gave a heavy sigh. "Just before you had the car accident I overheard you talking on the phone. I didn't mean to eavesdrop but when I heard what you were saying I couldn't turn away."

His frown deepened. "Ok. What did you hear?" He wasn't happy that he'd been spied on, even if it was Kirsty. Trust was an important issue to him.

"You said something about cut backs… are you planning to fire people in the New Year?"

Sean leaned back on the sofa and let out a sigh. "I wish you'd talked to me about this sooner. Of course I'm not firing people. The team I have are exceptional at what they do. I couldn't put them off even if I wanted to. Without you all the magazine would fall on its ear."

Kirsty looked confused. "Then I don't understand."

"I put it to the hierarchy to take a salary cut. We earn more than we need and it would boost the finances of the business, which we agreed upon. Was this the reason for the initial brush off?" She had canceled their first dinner date because of what she'd overheard, he now realized.

"Uh, well, yes, kind of." She shifted on the sofa feeling uncomfortable now.

"You know you should've turned and walked away. Listening in on other people's conversations is a violation of trust."

"Yes, I do. And if I could go back and change it I would."

Sean stood up and crossed the room to the unlit fireplace, leaning against the mantel. "Your admission changes things between us. How can I trust you now?"

Kirsty popped up off the sofa and rushed over to him. "It doesn't have to. You can trust me. If I hadn't told you things would still be the same."

He frowned into her hazel colored eyes. "Yes, they would, but there would be an issue of trust, wouldn't there? Did you feel guilty about what you'd done?"

"Yes, of course I did, but…"

"Then you know the answer to your next question."

"Please, Sean, I'm sorry. Don't do this."

"I'm sorry too." He stared into her glistening eyes for a moment, then crossed the room, opened the door and stepped outside. He'd had his heart broken by trusting too much and wouldn't allow it to happen again. If he couldn't trust the woman he loved with the little things how could he trust her with the bigger things?

Tears welled in Kirsty's eyes and she sobbed. How could he not give her time to explain?

A knock echoed into the room and the door opened. Allie's face appeared around the edge of the door. When she saw Kirsty crying she closed the door and rushed over to her, hugging her tight. "What happened, honey? Sean looks upset." She frowned at her friend. "So do you."

"I told him and he said I violated his trust." She sobbed against her friend's chest. "He doesn't want to be with me anymore."

"Oh, honey, I'm so sorry. If I'd known what would happen I wouldn't have pushed you to do it."

"It's my fault. I should've asked him months ago. He's right. I did violate his trust."

"Maybe, yeah, but is that any reason to break up? Couldn't he have worked it out with you?"

"He's a man with strong principals, Allie."

"I get that, but…"

"I blew it. He's never going to trust me again. I might even lose my job over this."

"No. He wouldn't do that." Allie shook her head, even though she wasn't at all sure.

Chapter Ten

THREE MONTHS LATER

Kirsty had been unable to stay with the magazine, even though she loved her job. Working with Sean, knowing how he felt about her would have been too difficult so she had made the decision to move on to something new. She had handed in her resignation a few days after the New Year's Eve party, and to her surprise, Sean didn't bat an eyelid over it. He'd wished her well and had left it at that.

She'd started her own Fashion For The Fuller Figure blog several months before as a side hustle (which she was grateful for now) and also a podcast which were both doing exceptionally well. Paid the bills and then some. It was her fresh start and she was grateful for it. It felt good to be doing something that would help make a difference in the lives of women, who for far too long, had been told to lose weight and not to wear certain clothing items. She hadn't always been as slim as she was now. In fact, in high school kids used to call her Tubby. Not nice, but kids will be kids.

She was working out of the spare bedroom which she had turned into an office, saved on rent somewhere else, and her overheads were low. She felt free for the first time in a long while and loved it.

A knock echoed into her apartment and she got up from her desk, walked out and crossed the living room and opened the door. It was her best friend, Allie.

The women hugged.

"Hey, how are you?" Kirsty motioned for her friend to come in.

"I'm good. How about you?"

"I'm great." Kirsty's face lit up.

"I can tell. Congrats on the new adventure. I hope you're going great with it."

"I am." She closed the door. "Want some coffee?"

"Sure." Allie crossed the living room and sat down at the dining table.

Kirsty brought the mugs in and set one down in front of Allie then took her seat opposite. "So are you on a day off?"

"Yeah. And I thought why not drop by to see how you're doing."

"I appreciate it. You know you can come by anytime."

"I know." Allie took a cautious sip of her coffee.

"Is something wrong?"

"No, of course not. Can't a friend visit a friend without a reason?"

"Sure you can." Kirsty smiled. She had a feeling something was wrong but wouldn't push it. If Allie wanted to talk about it she would.

"So what are your next plans?"

"I'm comfortable where I am at the moment, so I don't have any."

Allie looked uncomfortable all of a sudden.

"What is it?"

"Nothing."

"Come on, Al, I know you too well. What's going on?"

Her friend didn't speak for a moment. "Sean's got a new girlfriend."

Kirsty almost spat her coffee all over the table cloth. "Well, it was bound to happen sometime. He's single."

"Yeah. The only thing is she looks a lot like you."

"What?"

Allie pulled her phone from her purse and scrolled through the photos. "Here. See." She turned the phone around for Kirsty to see.

71

"Oh."

"He's clearly not over you, Kirst. He's only been dating her for about a month so…"

Kirsty shook her head. "No. It's done. He made the mistake of ending it before it even got started and that was his choice. If he regrets that decision he has to live with it now."

"But…" Allie knew they should be together.

Kirsty raised her hand. "Allie, it's over. It has been for months. Good luck to him."

Allie sighed. "Ok. But I think you should talk to him, see if he's had a change of heart."

"He hasn't. If he did he'd be calling me."

"I suppose you're right." Allie sipped her coffee. "It's just…"

"Please, Al, let's just leave it at that. Ok?"

Allie nodded. "If that's what you want?"

"It is. My life has changed. I'm happy. I don't need past mistakes ruining that."

"Ok."

Kirsty stood up. "Want a cookie to go with the coffee?"

"Sure, why not."

In the kitchen, a single tear slipped down Kirsty's right cheek. Underneath, she had missed Sean and wondered how he was doing. Allie knew not to talk about him when they got together so she hadn't heard about the new girlfriend until now. Oh well, they were both single, as she'd said, it was his choice who he dated.

Later the same afternoon, Kirsty made a trip into the city to buy some stationery items she needed at City Papery. It was the beginning of spring and the weather was lovely: a warm gentle breeze, blue sky dotted with fluffy white clouds. What more could you ask for in a perfect day? After picking up what she needed, Kirsty headed to a nearby coffee shop, sat down at an outdoor table, and checked her stats for the new blog she'd posted in the morning. She smiled, but the smile disappeared when she recognized the voice.

"Well hello."

"Sean?" She inhaled a quiet gasp of surprise. Of all the people she could run into, why him?

"How are you?"

His manner toward her was cordial but matter-of-fact and Kirsty wondered why he'd even bothered to speak to her at all.

"I'm well. You?"

"Can't complain. I heard you have a fashion blog and a podcast channel these days."

"Yes, I do."

"How's that working for you?"

"Very well, actually. The blog and the podcast are quite popular."

"Good to hear." His gaze shifted to the café doorway as his girlfriend came out with two coffees in hand. "Charlie, this is Kirsty. Kirsty, Charlie."

"Nice to meet you," the young woman said, handing a coffee to Sean.

"Yes, you too." Kirsty's gaze moved from her to him. "Well, I'd better let you go. Good to see you again. Take care." She gave them a thin smile.

"You too." He slipped an arm around the woman and they walked off down the sidewalk.

Kirsty let out the breath she hadn't realized she'd been holding. First, Allie came over to tell her Sean had a new girlfriend, then she runs into them together. Why? And her friend had been correct. Charlie did resemble her.

Maybe it was time to take a trip home to see her family. She could use the support right now. And it would be wonderful to finally meet her nephew, Gabriel. She'd been meaning to get back before now, but getting her business off the ground had to come first. She made the decision to call her mom the moment she stepped through the front

74

door of her apartment and to pack and be ready to leave the following morning.

The drive out there would help clear her head and by the time she arrived she'd be relaxed and ready to enjoy some quality time with the people she loved.

CHAPTER ELEVEN

Christine came out to greet her daughter as she pulled her car into the drive. "Hello, hello. It's so good to have you home. She wrapped her arms around Kirsty in a tight welcoming hug. "How was the trip?"

"Good." Kirsty walked to the back of her hatchback and lifted the door. "The roads were mostly empty and it's such a beautiful day. She tugged her suitcase from the trunk and closed it.

"Your sister is coming over later. She can't wait for you to meet Gabriel."

"I'm so excited." Kirsty pulled the handle up on her wheelie suitcase and followed her mother into the house.

"Want some coffee?"

"Sure. I'll just take my luggage upstairs and be right down." Kirsty headed for the stairs.

"I'll be in the kitchen," her mother called.

Within minutes, Kirsty was back and sitting at the center counter with her mom eating cookies and drinking coffee, talking and laughing. It felt like the perfect pick-me-up after everything that had happened over the past few months.

Christine watched her daughter for a moment. There was a kind of sadness behind her eyes. Should she ask? "So how's work? How's Allie? We haven't seen her in a while."

Kirsty hadn't told her parents she'd left the magazine. Something she'd known she would have to do eventually. "Um, work's good. Busy. And Allie's doing great. I just saw her yesterday."

"Oh, that's good to hear. Maybe she can come for a visit the next time you come home."

"I'll definitely ask her." Kirsty gave a thin smile.

Christine frowned. "Is everything all right?" She reached across the counter and took her daughter's hand in hers.

"Of course." Kirsty shrugged. "Why wouldn't it be?"

"I don't know. But it seems like there's something on your mind."

Kirsty had always been in awe of how her mom could suss out these kinds of things with all of them.

"I have to tell you something."

"Ok," Christine said gently.

"I quit the magazine and started my own business. I have a blog and a podcast that are doing really well. Pays the bills."

"As long as you're happy that's all that matters. Are you?"

"I think so."

"What made you make the change?"

Kirsty swallowed. "A few things, actually. I got involved with my boss and it didn't work out. And I was in need of a change. I felt bogged down."

"Oh, honey, I'm sorry things didn't work out." She rubbed her daughter's hand and gave her a pained look. "But you're happy now and doing well, that's what counts." She smiled.

"Yes, exactly."

"Do you want to talk about what happened?"

At that moment, the front door opened and Kristen came into the entry hall. "Hello," she called.

Christine and Kirsty climbed off the stools they were sitting on and hurried into the hallway.

"Hey, Sis," Kirsty greeted, stepping up and giving her sister a tight hug.

"Hey, yourself." Kristen eased out of her sister's embrace. "This darling little fellow is your nephew." She unclipped the harness, lifted her son out of his pram and handed him to Kirsty.

Tears welled in her eyes as she ran her gaze over the three month old, rosy-cheeked cherub in her arms. "Hey, little guy. I'm your Aunt Kirsty. It's so great to meet you." She planted a soft kiss on his forehead and looked at her sister. "I'm sorry I couldn't get back any sooner."

"It's ok. I know how busy you are. Don't stress."

"Let's go sit down in the living room," Christine said.

The three women entered the room, Kirsty sitting on the sofa with her sister and their mother sitting in an armchair across the coffee table from them.

"I've loved getting all the wonderful photos of Gabriel. I have so many of them on my refrigerator door." She bounced the baby on her knee, making funny faces at him.

"They change so fast. It's hard to remember him as a newborn already. I have to go back and look at the photos myself." Kristen smiled at her sister then at Gabriel who was also smiling.

Christine sat across from her girls and grandson and smiled. This was what family was all about. "Do you girls want a snack, coffee, tea?"

Kristen looked at her. "That would be great, Mom. Thank you."

Christine stood up. "Want to join me in the kitchen?"

The sisters stood and followed their mother into the bright, large workspace.

"Where's Dad?" Kristen asked.

"He went into town to the hardware store. He's got a new project happening. Don't ask me what it is because I have no idea. I guess I'll get to see it when it's finished." Christine busied herself with preparing food and pouring more coffee.

Kirsty and Kristen climbed onto stools at the center counter, Gabriel gurgling and smiling as he sat on the countertop in front of his aunt.

"He's almost due for a feed and a nap," Kristen told her sister.

"Oh, ok, can I feed him?"

Kristen chuckled. "Not unless you have milk in those boobs."

Kirsty grinned and handed her nephew to his mother. "Oh."

The women sat together talking, laughing and reminiscing while Kristen fed her son and put him down for a sleep, wheeling the baby carriage across the hall into the living room so he wouldn't be disturbed by their chatter.

Once Kristen was back she asked, "So, how's your love life?"

Christine shook her head at her daughter and Kristen got the message.

"Uh, at the moment I don't have one."

"Ok. It would be nice for you though."

"Maybe some time in the future, but not right now."

"I worry about you." Kristen frowned into her sister's eyes. "You should be dating and having fun."

"I'm too busy at the moment."

"Kirsty has a new business venture going," Christine chimed in, trying to steer the conversation away from romance and relationships.

Kristen's right eyebrow arched. "Oh? What kind of business venture? I thought you loved working at the magazine."

"I did. But it was time for a change."

"So tell me all about it." Kristen smiled.

Later that night, as Kirsty lay in her childhood bed she wondered about what Allie had said about Sean. His new girlfriend's resemblance to her was uncanny… a little spooky, in fact. Did he still have feelings for her? She knew she still had feelings for him, no matter how hard she tried not to. She couldn't just turn them off like a light switch.

She knew her mom would ask again at some point. And she knew she would have to tell her what happened to break them up. Would her mother be disappointed in her? She and her sister had been raised to be honest and trustworthy. She hoped her mom would understand that she had been only looking out for the people she worked with, concerned for their well-being.

Kirsty sighed and turned over, gazing out of the window at the twinkling stars in the blue black clear night sky, and made a silent wish. The line from the Disney song, *When you wish upon a star your dreams come true*, popped into her head and she hoped that what she had wished for *would* come true.

CHAPTER TWELVE

After spending the weekend with her family, Kirsty felt refreshed and ready to skyrocket her blog and podcast into the fashion world hemisphere. People were loving what she wrote and posted on YouTube and she was grateful that her business plan was taking off. Working for herself turned out to be more rewarding than she could have possibly imagined, and every day she felt as though she had accomplished something amazing for herself and the thousands of women out there that were taken for granted because of their size.

She had teed up some interviews with plus-sized, well-known figures of the community and beyond, lining up models and actresses to talk on her podcast about how they overcame the stigma of being a plus-size. She wanted women to feel good about themselves, not be torn down by other women… and men who had been brainwashed by societal standards of how a woman should look and dress.

As she sat at her desk, putting the finishing touches to her latest blog, her cell jingled in the living room. Getting to her feet and stretching, Kirsty headed to the other room, snatched up her phone from the coffee table and checked the caller ID. Unknown number. Perhaps it was one of her upcoming guests. She pressed the button. "Hello?"

Silence.

Kirsty tugged the phone from her ear and frowned at the screen, then pressed it to her ear again. "Hello?"

"Kirsty."

Her stomach went hollow.

"Sean?"

"Hi, yes."

"Why are you calling me?"

"I… can we meet?"

"Why?" A shiver ran through her and she shrugged off the uncomfortable feeling.

"I'd like to run something by you."

"Work related?"

"Yes. Do you have time?"

Kirsty swallowed hard. "Not right now."

"That's fine. When would suit you? Can you come into the office?"

"I'd prefer not to."

"I understand. How about Coffee Project on east Fifth Street?"

"Sounds better. When?"

"When do you have time?"

Kirsty gave it some thought. She could always say no. But she wanted to see him. "Tomorrow, say around ten?"

"Ok. Ten sounds good. See you then." Silence again. "Thank you. I appreciate your time."

"No problem." Kirsty rang off, her stomach flipping over beneath the elastic waistband of her pajamas. She liked working from home because she could relax and stay in her pajamas if she liked. Which she did. Why had Sean gotten in touch with her? What did he want to discuss that was work related? She would just have to wait until tomorrow to find out.

For the rest of the day, she found it hard to concentrate. She kept making stupid mistakes and became frustrated with everything she did. Giving a heavy sigh, she decided to call it quits for the day. She'd make a coffee, veg out on the sofa and watch a couple of movies in the hope they would take her mind off Sean. Was his call an excuse to see her again? Had Allie been right when she said she thought he still had feelings for her? But what about his new girlfriend, Charlie? She'd be the one to get hurt out of all this. She was getting way too far ahead of herself. *Wait and see what he wants first*, she counselled.

Kirsty had to admit to herself that she'd been in love with him at the time of their break up. She had done all she could not to fall for Sean, but it had been so easy because he was the complete package: tall, dark and handsome. Financially secure. Spoke several languages. Well traveled. She knew it was a cliché, but he was. And she could always read what was going on in his gorgeous blue eyes.

She brought her coffee into the living room, set the mug down on the coffee table, crawled onto the sofa, picked up the remote and turned on the TV. Netflix was sure to have something to watch. She scrolled through the assortment of movies, picked a romantic comedy and settled back to be entertained and taken to another place for a while. She really didn't want to think about Sean anymore for the rest of the night.

After an hour or so, a knock echoed into the living room and Kirsty paused the movie to go answer it. When she checked through the peephole, her stomach squeezed tight. She eased the door back. "What are you doing here?"

"I couldn't wait until tomorrow. I needed to see you today." He motioned to the inside of her apartment. "May I come in? I won't stay long."

Kirsty let out a sigh and stepped aside. "Sure."

"Thank you." His blue eyes met hers and he gave her a thin smile.

"Have a seat." Kirsty closed the door and followed him across to the dining room table.

"Thanks." He sat down opposite her. "I appreciate you seeing me impromptu."

"Well, you gave me no choice. Here you are."

"I'm sorry."

"What's going on, Sean?" She shifted uncomfortably on her chair. "I don't see or hear from you in months and now you're calling me and coming here. Why?"

"I – I know." He sighed. "Things haven't been the same since you left." He raised his hand when she opened her mouth to speak. "I know I was the one to end things, but…"

"You have a girlfriend now, Sean."

"No, I don't. We ended it."

"We? Or you? What did she do to make you change your mind about her?" She gave him a stern stare.

"I suppose I deserve that. She did nothing. She realized I was still in love with you." There, it was out in the open.

Kirsty sat gobsmacked not knowing what to say. He was in love with her. She wanted to be happy about it but something prevented it.

"I know I should've given you the benefit of the doubt back then. I realize you were only looking out for the people you cared about. I made a hasty decision that I now regret."

She frowned. "Why did you break up with me?"

"I'd had my heart broken and found it difficult to trust again."

"I'm sorry."

"I was engaged to be married a few years ago and my then fiancée ran off with another man. Someone she'd been having an affair with for months. Someone she had worked with."

"That's… I'm so sorry. But I'm not her. I would never do something like that to you."

"It took a while for me to figure that out. I'm sorry it's taken this long."

"What do you expect me to do with all of this information?"

"I hope you'll consider giving me another chance. I don't expect you to say anything right now, just think it over. Give it some time to see how you really feel."

Kirsty had conflicted emotions. She'd dreamed of Sean coming to her and professing his undying love, but now that he was here she wasn't sure how she felt about it. "Ok. You're right. I'll need some time."

"Fair enough." He stood up. "Thank you for hearing me out. I'll hear from you?"

"You will." She nodded, crossed the living room and opened the door.

Sean stood looking down at her. He wanted to kiss her but wouldn't dare. She needed time, as she'd said. "Ok, well, bye for now." He stepped out into the hallway.

"Yes." Kirsty closed the door and leaned against it, letting out a huge sigh. Had there been a business proposition he wanted to discuss or was it just a ploy to meet? She gave another sigh as she realized her wish had come true, but what was she going to do about it now?

CHAPTER THIRTEEN

A week went by without Kirsty getting in touch with Sean. He had given her the space she had asked for, and she had given their possible relationship a lot of serious thought, wondering if things would be different now that she knew what had happened to make him not trust her. Her heart was urging her to call him, but her head was saying be careful. His dismissal of her the evening of the New Year's Eve party hurt and she knew she wouldn't want to go through the same pain again. Could she trust him?

After finishing off her new blog post and uploading the latest podcast, Kirsty decided to give him a call to see if he wanted to meet for dinner, so they could talk. "Hi, can you meet me for dinner?"

"Of course. Where'd you have in mind?"

"How about the Sea Fire Grill on east 48th street? Do you know it?"

"I do. What time?"

"Oh, say, seven?"

"Seven sounds great. I'll see you then." He would've liked to pick her up but thought it too soon to offer.

"Ok. See you there."

"And, Kirsty…"

"Yes?"

"Thank you."

"I'll see you later." She rang off, her heart skipping nervously in her chest.

The restaurant had an elegant ambience. Cream and wood chairs with white covered tables. The mood was subdued in the first section of the restaurant with subtle lighting, dark wood bar, and the right hand wall lined with filled wine racks. Further through, the back area of the place was well lit with a wooden parquet floor, and there was also a private dining room for other functions. She had asked for a table at the back right hand corner as she knew the popular restaurant would be quite busy, and it would allow them a small amount of privacy.

As she walked to their table, Sean was waiting for her and stood up when she approached.

"Good to see you," he greeted with a smile, came around the table and pulled out her chair for her.

"Thank you," she said.

"You look lovely tonight."

"I appreciate that. You look nice too." She smiled and sat down, hanging her evening shoulder purse on the back of the chair.

Sean took his seat again. "Would you like some wine?" He'd ordered a bottle and had a glass in front of him.

"Yes, thanks." Butterflies danced in the pit of her stomach and she attempted to relax. Perhaps the wine would help with that.

"How was your day?" he asked.

"Good. Busy. Yours?"

"Yes, busy but productive."

Kirsty picked up a menu to peruse. "It all sounds so good."

"Hungry?"

"Yes."

"Me too. And it's on me."

"Oh no…"

He raised a hand. "It's fine. I'd like to buy you dinner."

Kirsty decided not to resist. "Ok, great."

"Order anything you like."

"Thanks." Her eyes roamed the selections on the menu.

As the evening progressed, with the conversation mostly small talk, Kirsty broached the topic of why they were there. "I think we should talk, Sean."

"I thought we were." He gave her a thin smile and picked up his wine glass, swallowing a large mouthful of the gold colored liquid.

"I mean about us." She shifted on her chair and smoothed out her red dress.

"Ok. What do you want to say?"

"I understand now why you were so quick to push me away. You'd been hurt… badly… and it made it difficult for you to trust again. But I'm not your ex-fiancée, Sean, I wouldn't do what she did to you. I am honest, and I am loyal… despite the stupid mistake I made by listening in on a private conversation."

He reached across and took her hand in his. "I realize that… and I'm sorry for what I put you through. What I put us both through. I've missed you."

She wanted to say she'd missed him, and she had, but she needed to stay strong for the moment, to let him see she wouldn't go through what he'd put her through again. "I know. But I won't be treated that way. Not again. You have to be able to trust me without wondering if you can."

"I can."

"Are you sure?"

He nodded. "Yes, very sure. I don't want to lose you again."

"Ok. We need to start slow and see how things go over time. Are you prepared to do that?"

"I'm happy to do whatever it takes for you to be comfortable with our relationship again." He squeezed her hand gently. "I love you, Kirsty."

She blinked away the tears stinging the backs of her eyes. She wanted to say those words, she did, but couldn't until she knew for sure their relationship was in a good place. "I'm not ready to say that yet."

"That's ok. Whenever you feel you can is fine with me."

Kirsty stepped into her apartment, kicked off her glossy black stilettos, leaving them by the door, and wandered through the dimly lit room to her bedroom to get ready for bed. The evening had gone well, she thought, and although she hadn't said she loved Sean, as he had her, she knew deep down that she did.

Climbing into bed, she exhaled a soft sigh and glanced out of her bedroom window. A bright star shone in the center of the pane of glass and she wondered if it was the same star she'd made the wish on at her parents' home only days before. Probably not, but it was a nice idea. As she drifted off to sleep, she thought about Sean and wondered if he was thinking about her. This time, she hoped things would work out between them because she really believed that he was the one for her.

CHAPTER FOURTEEN

THREE DAYS BEFORE CHRISTMAS

Kirsty packed the rest of her clothes and accessories into her suitcase, zipped it up, and stood it by the front door next to the huge bag of gifts. Tomorrow she and Sean would head out of the city and travel to her parents' home for the holidays. She was overjoyed to be spending time with her family again and to introduce Sean to them all, in the flesh, so to speak. They had gotten to know him via Zoom and had grown to love him just as much as she did. It was going to be an extra wonderful time of year, this year, she could feel it.

Over the past several months, Sean had proved to her many times over that she had made the right decision to give their relationship another try. He was kind, loving, generous, and made her feel like she was his special lady, which she was, and she couldn't be happier. As she sat and sipped eggnog, her cell jingled its usual holiday tune – Deck the Halls – and she picked it up from off the coffee table. "Hey, you, how's things?"

Allie gushed. "Eric asked me to marry him!" She squealed into the phone. "I'm sending you a pic of the ring."

Kirsty's text messages buzzed and she swiped the screen. "Oh my! That's gorgeous. Congratulations, sweetie. What a wonderful Christmas gift."

"Isn't it? I'm so happy."

"And I'm so happy for you."

"Are you heading out tomorrow?"

"Yes, we are."

"Well, safe travels. And remember not to open your present until midday Christmas Day."

"I won't. Promise. And the same goes for you. It's our tradition."

"I wouldn't dream of it. Have fun. I'll see you when you're back in town."

"Have a safe and very happy Christmas, my friend. Love you."

"Love you too." Allie rang off.

Kirsty sat smiling. She couldn't wipe the smile off her face if she tried. She was so happy for Allie. Eric was a good guy, a sweet man, and she knew they'd be happy together.

Heading into the kitchen, she rinsed her Christmas mug and sat it in the dish rack, then walked through the living room to her bedroom and climbed into bed. She was looking forward to the drive with Sean and to her family meeting him. Nothing could spoil the holidays for her, absolutely nothing. She lay back on her pillows and gazed up at the ceiling with a smile on her face. This would be their best Christmas ever.

As she drifted off to sleep, her cell jingled on the bedside table. She jabbed her fingers across the wooden surface, her eyes still closed, feeling for the offending phone making the offending noise. She needed sleep. Finding the phone, she snatched it up, drew it to her face and checked the caller ID. Sean.

"Hey, what's up?" She was well awake now and sitting up in bed.

"Sweetheart, I hate to do this but I'm going to have to follow you out to your parents'."

"Oh no. Why? What's happened?" Kirsty swung her legs over the side of the bed, stood up and walked over to the window. A light dusting of snow sat on the windowsill outside.

"We've had a major glitch in the printing press. I've

got people working on it but it looks like it's going to run into tomorrow. I'm so sorry about this, but as soon as it's fixed I'll be on my way to you."

She was so looking forward to the drive with him. It wouldn't be the same, but there was nothing she could do. "It's not your fault. It's just…"

"I know. I was looking forward to the drive together too. I will be there. I promise."

"Ok. Just don't rush to get there. Be safe on the road."

"I will. I have to go. I love you."

"I love you too." She let out a disappointed sigh as she rang off, pushed the phone onto the bedside table, climbed back under the covers, and turned over. *What bad timing.*

More snow had begun to fall, giving the atmosphere a real holiday feel. Christmas was her favorite time of the year and she hoped it would all work out the way she wanted it to.

Pulling into her parents' driveway, Kirsty turned off the engine and sat for a moment. She'd let her mom know Sean would be arriving later, so there was no need for explanations now. As she stepped out of the car, the front door opened and her sister Kristen came out onto the porch carrying Gabriel on her hip.

"Hey, you. Glad you're here," Kristen greeted.

"Me too. Boy it's cold."

"Yeah, more so than last Christmas."

Kirsty tugged her case from the trunk, closed the hatch and climbed the front steps. "Where's mom and dad?"

"They went into town for some last minute shopping." Kristen stepped inside. "Come on in, it's freezing out there."

Kirsty set her wheelie case by the front door and headed into the living room to the roaring fire, reaching out her hands to warm them up. "Brady at work?"

"Yeah, he'll be here later for dinner. Will Sean get here today?"

"He hopes so. He said he would, unless something doesn't go according to plan." Kirsty walked over to her sister. "Hand over the cutie." She held out her arms for her nephew. "Hey, buddy, how're you doing?" She planted a kiss on his rosy cheek. "Teething?"

"Yes. He's ok for the moment, but it's hard at night."

"I can't even imagine."

The pair went into the kitchen, Kirsty climbing onto a stool at the center counter while her sister poured coffee and plated up some brownies. Bringing the plate over, she set it down in the center of the counter, grabbed the two mugs of coffee and joined Kirsty.

"I'm so glad you've met a good man," Kristen said. "It's nice for you."

"Thanks. Yes, it is nice." She took a sip of the steaming coffee.

"Any thoughts of marriage?"

Kirsty almost choked on the mouthful of coffee. "No. We haven't been dating that long."

Her sister shrugged. "You love each other so what's the problem?"

"Hey, I'm glad you're in a happy marriage, but it's not something I want to think about right now. Maybe one day."

"Ok. You're right."

Gabriel sat on the countertop in front of Kirsty gurgling and smiling at her. "He's such a cute little guy."

"Well, like I said. You could have one of your own."

"Kristen."

"What? It's true."

"Let's talk about something else, ok?"

"Whatever you say." She chuckled.

"Mind if I hand Gabriel back and head upstairs? I want to unpack and change."

"Sure, no problem." She took Gabriel and sat him in his pram beside her. "We'll still be here when you come back down. Maybe mom and dad too."

101

"Cool." Kirsty grabbed her case and climbed the stairs.

In her room, she opened up her case and pulled out the drawers of the dresser, placing her folded things inside. Once unpacked, and changed into something more comfortable, she slid the case under the bed and headed back downstairs.

When she reached the bottom of the staircase, the front door opened and her parents stepped into the entry hall.

"Hi, Mom, Dad," Kirsty greeted, walking over and giving them both a hug.

Hi, sweetheart. I'm glad you're here," Christine said with a smile.

Hey, sweet pea. Good to see ya." Her dad wrapped his arms around her.

"Have you had a snack?" her mom asked.

"Yep. Kristen's been the perfect host." Kirsty smiled and pointed to the kitchen.

The three walked into the large workspace.

"Hey, Mom, Dad," Kristen said. "Get everything you needed?"

"We did." Her dad popped the shopping bags onto the counter near the sink and started putting things away.

"Honey, what time will Sean get here?" Christine asked.

"I'm not sure. He said he'd call when the repairs were

completed, so I guess they're still ongoing." She sighed.

"Oh ok. I hope he gets here before nightfall. The forecast is for heavy snow. If it gets too bad they'll detour the traffic and he might have to stay over somewhere until tomorrow."

Chapter Fifteen

Early the next morning, Kirsty's cell woke her with a jolt. She scrambled up in bed, reached for her phone and checked the screen. Sean. "Hey, are you on your way?" He'd been held up the previous day with the repairs and had called to let her know he'd be arriving the following afternoon. Nothing had gone according to plan so far, and Kirsty wanted to believe things would only get better from here as it was Christmas Eve.

"Hey. I hope to clear the city in a few hours. The repairs have taken longer than expected due to some kind of technical glitch that couldn't be located at first. I'm sorry things haven't gone the way we'd hoped, but I plan to make it up to you."

Kirsty gave a soft sigh. It wasn't Sean's fault the magazine's computer system was in bad need of an upgrade. "I hope it all works out and you can get on the road soon."

"Me too. I'm looking forward to meeting your family in person."

She threw back the warm covers and swung her legs over the side of the bed. "Please give me a call before you leave so I know you're on your way."

"I will. I've got to go. Love you."

"Love you too." Kirsty pushed her phone back onto the bedside table, got up and went to take a shower. She knew she'd feel more human afterward. She really needed to get into the Christmas spirit. The day would improve and Sean would get to her parents' before the end of the day.

When she came downstairs, her mom was in the kitchen making pancakes.

"Morning," Kirsty greeted.

"Morning, honey. How'd you sleep?" Christine flipped the golden pancake over in the pan.

"Good. I couldn't get off to sleep right away because I was worried about Sean, but once I spoke to him I drifted right off."

"He'll be here today then?"

"He said he should clear the city this afternoon."

"Your dad and I are so looking forward to finally meeting him in person. It's been nice and all having the chats online via Zoom, but nothing can make up for actually spending time with someone."

105

"I know what you mean. And Sean's looking forward to it too."

"Sit. Eat." Christine brought the plate of hot pancakes over to the counter and climbed onto a tall stool.

"Where's dad?" Kirsty asked, forking a couple of pancakes onto her plate.

"Where do you think?"

"In his workshop?"

"You guessed it."

"What's he doing out there?"

Christine shrugged. "A secret project is all he told me."

"Oh? I wonder what it is."

"I guess we'll find out soon enough."

Mother and daughter sat together eating pancakes with butter and maple syrup, and discussed the Christmas Day festivities. Kirsty couldn't wait. She loved the holidays, opening presents, spending time with the people she loved, watching old Christmas movies… and drinking her mom's famous eggnog. It was always a treat.

As the day rolled on, Kirsty was worried because she hadn't heard from Sean as he'd promised. She'd left him a couple of text messages and, on checking, found he hadn't replied. Was he on the road? Could he be in a low reception area right now?

Kirsty wandered into the kitchen.

Her mom was busy prepping the turkey for tomorrow's Christmas dinner.

"Can I help with anything?" she offered, climbing onto a stool.

"No, but thanks, I think I've got everything covered." She smiled and brushed some stray strands of her brunette hair off her forehead. "You could pour us some coffee though."

"Ok, sure." Kirsty climbed off the stool, opened an overhead cupboard, took out two holiday mugs and poured coffee into each, setting one down for her mom on the center counter.

"Thanks, hon." Christine took a seat.

"Are Kristen and Brady coming over later for the movies?"

"Your sister texted me a while ago and said that Gabriel is having a rough day. Teething. But they would try to make it."

Kirsty gave her mom a pained look. "Oh, poor little guy. I hope he'll be ok. And I hope they can make it, but if not, at least we'll see them tomorrow." She remembered the presents in the trunk of her car. "After our coffee would you come out and help me bring in the gifts from my car?"

"Of course, honey. We can sit them under the tree in the living room."

"Yes…" Her phone went off in her shirt pocket and she plucked it out. "It's Sean." She stepped down off the stool, crossed the entry hall and walked into the living room. "Hey, how's things?"

"I'm just about ready to leave. Sorry for not getting back to you, things have been a little crazy around here."

Kirsty's face brightened. "Oh, that's good news. It's ok. I was a little worried, but I thought things would work out. Did the technician get everything sorted?"

"Yes, he did. So the first edition for the new year will run on time."

"I'm so glad." She walked over to the seven foot tree standing in the corner of the room and her gaze moved up the twinkling lights and decorations to the star on top. "I can't wait to see you. I've missed you."

"I've missed you too. I should be there around six, seven at the latest."

"Ok. Please drive safe and I'll see you when you get here."

"I will. Bye for now. Love you."

"Love you too." She rang off and smiled. She liked telling him she loved him and she liked hearing it as well.

As she walked back into the kitchen, her mom's curious gaze met hers. "He's on his way?" Christine asked.

"Yeah, he is. He should arrive around six or seven tonight."

"Ok, well, we'll have a late dinner then."

"Oh, Mom, you don't have to do that. Just keep something for him to have when he gets here."

Her mom shook her head. "We'll all sit down together to eat. It would be rude not to. Besides, it's Christmas Eve."

Kirsty walked over and gave her mother a hug. "Thank you."

"No need to thank me, honey. It's the right thing to do."

At seven thirty, a car pulled into the drive behind Kirsty's red Honda. Kirsty heard the rumble of the engine, tugged open the door and rushed outside into the freezing snow. As Sean climbed out of his car, she threw her arms around his neck and planted a firm kiss on his lips. "I'm so glad you're here."

"Me too. The snow was getting heavier the last couple of miles. I'm glad to be off the road." He kissed her forehead. "It's freezing out here."

"Let's get your luggage inside." Kirsty walked to the trunk and Sean popped the lid. "Oh my." There were presents galore and one medium-sized suitcase.

"I couldn't come out here empty-handed, now could I?"

"It looks like you bought out the store," Kirsty quipped, giving him a huge smile. She bundled up a few packages and hurried inside to place the gifts under the tree, then returned to help Sean with the rest.

Once inside, Kirsty took Sean's hand and ushered him into the living room. "Uh, Mom, Dad, Sean's here."

Her mom and dad got up, crossed the living room and offered a warm welcome.

Kristen and Brady hadn't come over because of Gabriel, but would be arriving early for breakfast the next morning, Christmas morning.

The evening was perfect. Kirsty, Sean, and her parents had dinner together, then sat and watched Christmas movies, drank eggnog and got to know each other better.

Kirsty smiled as she watched Sean talking with her parents. They loved him. And so did she.

At around ten o'clock, Sean took her hand and asked her to go out onto the front porch with him. He wanted to speak to her about something.

Shivering in the chill air, Kirsty wondered why they had to talk outside.

"Come here," Sean said, smiling.

Kirsty walked up to him. "Is everything ok?" Butterflies danced in the pit of her stomach. She hoped so.

"Everything's perfect." He smiled down at her. "I love you so much. I know we got off to a rocky start…"

She placed her finger on his lips. "That's in the past. You've made me the happiest I've ever been, Sean Donovan. I couldn't ask for anyone better."

His smile widened and her heart fluttered in her chest.

"I'm glad to hear you say that because I'm the happiest I've ever been as well. You make me happy, Kirsty." He leaned in and kissed her forehead, then stepped back, tugged a small black box from the pocket of his navy overcoat.

Kirsty gasped and raised her hands to her mouth.

Sean got down on one knee and flipped the lid on the box open. Inside, nestled in white satin, sat the most beautiful ring she had ever laid eyes on. "I don't want to waste any more time. I love you and I know you love me so… Kirsty Holloway… will you marry me?"

Tears glistened in her eyes as Sean waited for her answer. "Yes, of course I'll marry you."

Sean slipped the solitary square cut diamond ring onto her finger. "You've made me the happiest man alive tonight." He leaned in and planted a long, firm kiss on her trembling lips.

She wrapped her arms around him and held him tight. "I'm so happy."

He eased her away from him. "Do you want to go in and tell your parents?"

"Not right now. I just want to have this moment with you alone."

"Ok."

The pair stood together on the front porch watching the snow fall. It was a magical moment.

A few minutes later, the front door opened and Kirsty's dad stuck his head outside. "Hey, it's freezing out here, are you two coming in soon? Christine's making hot chocolate with marshmallows."

Kirsty turned to look at him. "We'll be in in a minute, Dad."

"Ok. I'll leave you to it then." He closed the door.

"It is getting even colder out here now," Sean observed.

"Yes, I can't feel my face." Kirsty chuckled. "Let's go in and tell them the wonderful news."

After taking off their coats, Kirsty and Sean went into the kitchen.

"Mom, Dad?"

Her parents turned around. "What is it, honey?" Christine asked.

Kirsty raised her left hand to display the engagement ring. "Sean asked me to marry him."

Her parents rushed over to the pair.

"Congratulations," they said together, their faces beaming.

"What wonderful news on such a magical night," her mother said. "We couldn't be happier for you both."

Later on in the evening, after her parents retired, Kirsty and Sean sat in front of the fire, arms around each other, watching the flames flickering in the fireplace. As he had said, they had gotten off to a rocky start, but had managed to find their way back to each other.

"I love you, Kirsty. You've made me so happy by saying yes."

"You made me happy asking me."

"Our life together is going to be amazing, I can feel it." Sean pulled her closer and kissed the top of her head.

Kirsty smiled up at him. She knew he was the right man for her. Had known it from the moment they'd sat together in that café not far from the Magazine's office after fixing the glitch in the system the previous Christmas holidays. "Well, of course it is. What more could you ask for than Christmas, mistletoe and me?" she joked, reaching around behind her, holding up a sprig of the white berried tree and planting a firm kiss on his smiling lips.

The Story of Mistletoe

Why do people kiss under the mistletoe?

Well, for centuries, mistletoe has been considered a plant that increases fertility and longevity. The Norse legend tells of Balder, son of Frigga the Norse Goddess of War and Sexuality, who was killed by an evil spirit with an arrow made of mistletoe.

Distraught by her son's death, Frigga wept and the red mistletoe berries turned white, which brought Balder back to life. Frigga was so overjoyed at her son's return that she blessed the plant, removing the evil from it, and promised a kiss to all who passed beneath it from that day forward.

In ancient times, visitors would kiss the hand of their host under the mistletoe when they arrived at their home as a way of honoring the legend. Since that time, the tradition has evolved into the Christmas custom everyone knows today: that if a woman is caught standing under the mistletoe she may receive a kiss from any man.

DID YOU ENJOY THIS NOVELLA?

Let other readers know by posting a
short review on Amazon.com

Visit the author's page
https://amzn.to/2wwbTr8